For Aunty Ann and Uncle Roy.
Thank you for always supporting
everything I do on my creative journey.
Lots of love xxx
- L.E.A.

BLOOMSBURY CHILDREN'S BOOKS
Bloomsbury Publishing Plc
50 Bedford Square, London, WC1B 3DP, UK

BLOOMSBURY, BLOOMSBURY CHILDREN'S BOOKS and the Diana logo are
trademarks of Bloomsbury Publishing Plc

First published in Great Britain 2020 by Bloomsbury Publishing Plc

Text and illustrations copyright © Laura Ellen Anderson 2020

Laura Ellen Anderson has asserted her rights under the Copyright,
Designs and Patents Act, 1988, to be identified as the Author and Illustrator of this work

A catalogue record for this book is available from the British Library

ISBN: HB: 978 1 5266 0245 9
PB: 978 1 5266 0244 2
eBook: 978 1 5266 0246 6

2 4 6 8 10 9 7 5 3 1

Printed and bound in by Leo Paper Products, Heshan, Guangdong

All papers used by Bloomsbury Publishing Plc are natural, recyclable products
from wood grown in well managed forests. The manufacturing
processes conform to the environmental regulations of the country of origin

To find out more about our authors and books visit www.bloomsbury.com and sign up for our newsletters

LAURA ELLEN ANDERSON

I DON'T WANT TO BE QUIET!

BLOOMSBURY
CHILDREN'S BOOKS

LONDON OXFORD NEW YORK NEW DELHI SYDNEY

OOOOOOOO!

I don't want
to be quiet,

I'd rather be

LOUD!

I want to be HEARD and
stand out from the crowd!

It's SO MUCH more fun,
when you're NOISY like ME . . .
But I don't understand
why Mum doesn't agree.

Mum whispers,
*"Be quiet, your brother
is sleeping."*

But, OOPS, it's too late,
now the baby is weeping.

At school I love

CHATTING
and
LAUGHING
and
CLAPPING,

but my teacher gets angry and then ends up **snapping.**

"ENOUGH, please be quiet!
You must **listen** in school."

But silence in class is a **terrible** rule!

Stairs are
for STOMPING,

BOSH

HOOPS

spoons are
for DRUMMING,

and when my mum's working,
I help her by HUMMING.

Food is for CRUNCHING

and drinks are for SLURPING.

QUIET PLEASE.

My feet are for SPLASHING,

my mouth is for BURPING (oops)!
BUT . . .

So, I make silly noises and shuffle my chair,
I twiddle my thumbs and fiddle my hair.

I huff and I puff and I finally BURST . . .

"SHHHHHHHHHHHHHHHHHHHHHHHHHHHHHHHHHHHHHH!"

says the WHOLE ROOM.
"No talking please!"

I stop . . . And I frown . . .
Then I stare at my knees.

My cheeks go all red, so I pick up a book -
maybe I'll give this a really quick look . . .

Page after page I read . . .
completely SPELLBOUND.

HOURS have passed, and
I've not made a SOUND.

But INSIDE my head there's a whole lot of NOISE -
magical quests - pirate girls and lost boys!

Next morning I LISTEN, and what do I hear?
Birds tweeting and singing their new morning cheer.

And then while at school
I learn lots of new things

about numbers

and poems

and the reign of
great kings.

I like being quiet,
it means I HEAR MORE
of the small gentle sounds
that I couldn't before . . .

But there are still LOTS of places and times to be LOUD . . .

When I'm
DRUMMING
and

DANCING

and . . .

TAP

TAP

making mum proud!